TOOTH ON THE LOOSE

Susan Middleton Elya

Illustrated by
Jenny Mattheson

G. P. Putnam's Sons

To Madison Wisconsin McAllaster Weaver and her mom, Katie—two good writers.
S.M.E.

For Will and Kamaile.
J.M.

G. P. PUTNAM'S SONS
A division of Penguin Young Readers Group.
Published by The Penguin Group.
Penguin Group (USA) Inc., 375 Hudson Street, New York, NY 10014, U.S.A.
Penguin Group (Canada), 90 Eglinton Avenue East, Suite 700, Toronto, Ontario M4P 2Y3, Canada (a division of Pearson Penguin Canada Inc.).
Penguin Books Ltd, 80 Strand, London WC2R 0RL, England.
Penguin Ireland, 25 St. Stephen's Green, Dublin 2, Ireland (a division of Penguin Books Ltd.).
Penguin Group (Australia), 250 Camberwell Road, Camberwell, Victoria 3124, Australia (a division of Pearson Australia Group Pty Ltd.).
Penguin Books India Pvt Ltd, 11 Community Centre, Panchsheel Park, New Delhi - 110 017, India.
Penguin Group (NZ), 67 Apollo Drive, Rosedale, North Shore 0632, New Zealand (a division of Pearson New Zealand Ltd.).
Penguin Books (South Africa) (Pty) Ltd, 24 Sturdee Avenue, Rosebank, Johannesburg 2196, South Africa.
Penguin Books Ltd, Registered Offices: 80 Strand, London WC2R 0RL, England.

Design by Richard Amari.
Text set in Goudy Sans.
The art was done in oil paint on primed paper.

Library of Congress Cataloging-in-Publication Data
Elya, Susan Middleton, 1955– Tooth on the loose / Susan Middleton Elya ; illustrated by Jenny Mattheson. p. cm. Summary: She would have some money if her wiggly tooth fell
out, and her father's birthday he would not go without, but the tooth is so stubborn and will not come out, so the gift for her father will be from a different route. Includes index of
Spanish words and phrases. [1. Teeth—Fiction. 2. Gifts—Fiction. 3. Spanish language—Fiction. 4. Stories in rhyme.] I. Mattheson, Jenny, ill. II. Title. PZ8.3.E514To 2008 [E]—dc22
2007007398

ISBN 978-0-399-24459-9
1 3 5 7 9 10 8 6 4 2

Glossary and Pronunciation Guide

Abuela (ah BWEH lah) Grandma

baños (BAH nyoce) baths

cabeza (kah BEH sah) head

chica (CHEE kah) girl

chicle (CHEE kleh) gum

cumpleaños (koom pleh AH nyoce) birthday

diente (DYEHN teh) tooth

dinero (dee NEH roe) money

el reloj (EHL rreh LOE) the clock

en frente (EHN FREHN teh) in front

espero (ehs PEH roe) I hope so

fiesta (FYEHS tah) party

hermano (ehr MAH noe) brother

la boca (LAH BOE kah) the mouth

la cena (LAH SEH nah) supper

leche (LEH cheh) milk

loca (LOE kah) crazy

maíz (mah EECE) corn

malo (MAH loe) bad

Mamá (mah MAH) Mom

manzana (mahn SAH nah) apple

mañana (mah NYAH nah) tomorrow

mascotas (mahs KOE tahs) pets

mesa (MEH sah) table

mi (MEE) my

Papá (pah PAH) Dad

papel (pah PEHL) paper

Papi (PAH pee) Daddy

perros (PEH rroce) dogs

poema (poe EH mah) poem

poeta (poe EH tah) poet

problema (proe BLEH mah) problem

regalo (rreh GAH loe) gift

rotas (RROE tahs) broken

silla (SEE yah) chair

sofá (soe FAH) couch

tarjeta (tahr HEH tah) card

te quiero (TEH KYEH roe) I love you

un dólar (OON DOE lahr) a dollar

My tooth is so wiggly,
I don't like to use it.
Papá says it won't be
too long till I lose it.

His birthday's tomorrow.
I have no **regalo**.
And that's not a good thing,
since *no gift* is **malo**!

My brother—**hermano**—
said, "**Chica**, good luck!
That tooth is worth money,
un dólar—a buck.

"The tooth fairy picks up
your tooth for her stash,
reminds you to floss,
then leaves you some cash."

I wiggled and poked it.
But it wasn't ready.
"I'll yank it!" my brother said.
"Try holding steady!"

I needed that tooth out
today, not **mañana**.
But yanking? Too painful.
I tried a **manzana**.

The apple was crunchy.
It hurt my loose **diente**,
since it was the one
right in front here—**en frente**.

"Eat sweet corn—**maíz**,"
suggested **Mamá**.

"Tie string to the doorknob," she said, "for **Papá**."

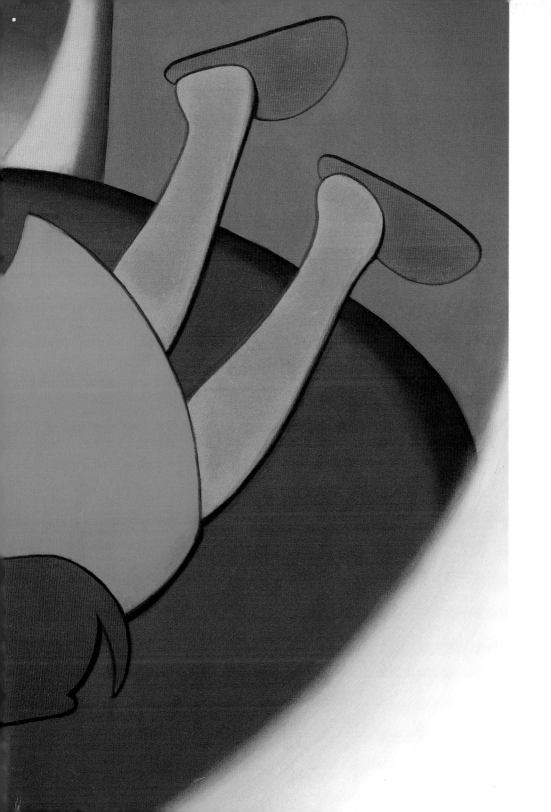

By bedtime, no luck,
so I wrote this **poema**:

*My movable tooth
is such a **problema**!*

*It just won't come out—
a pain in **la boca**.
It wiggles so much,
it's driving me **loca**!*

*Oh, when will I lose it?
I'm hoping—**espero**—
that it'll be soon,
since I need **dinero**!*

I woke to Dad's birthday.
No gift for **Papá**.
I looked for some coins
in the family **sofá**.

Instead of some money,
I found a small crumb,
a comb, and a pencil,
and **chicle**—old gum.

I tried to walk **perros**
and give puppies **baños**
to earn myself money
for Dad's **cumpleaños**!

But most of the pets
were unruly **mascotas**,
and money I earned
went to pay for things **rotas**.

The clock—**el reloj**—
was tick-tocking away.
And me with no present
and no way to pay.

Mamá said, "Don't fret that
there's nothing you bought.
The gift doesn't matter
as much as the thought."

"Supper! **¡La cena!**"
Abuela was calling.
"Come in the kitchen!"
I couldn't keep stalling.

I went to my **silla**
and sat at **la mesa**.
The others had presents.
I hung my **cabeza**.

Then in came **Papá**,
looking fine as can be.
He saw all the fuss,
said, "**Fiesta**, for me?"

"But first we'll eat supper,"
remarked **mi mamá**.
She winked as she showed me
her card for **Papá**.

I said, "I'll be back,"
and I dashed for the drawer
with paper—**papel**—
some markers and more.

I hid in the corner
and worked very hard
on a present to give him,
a poetry card:

*I have no **dinero**,
this card's all I've got.
But **Papi, te quiero**.
I love you a lot.*

*That's all! Gotta go
while **la cena** is hot.*

I gave him the card
and took a big bite.
Then out popped my **diente**,
so tiny and white.

Papá showed me how
to drink **leche** with style
with a straw through the hole
that was now in my smile.

Papá hung my card up,
my homemade **tarjeta**,
and told me that I am
his favorite **poeta**!